Patch of Happiness

NOEL LORENZ

facebook.com/countrygirrlpublishers

www.noellorenz.com

Title of Book: *Patch of Happiness*
Author of Book: Noel Lorenz
Series: Colors of My Heart, Book-9
First Published in India in Jan 2022 Country Girrl Publication
Cover Design: Copyright © Abhisek Ghosh, 2022.
Copyright © Abhisek Ghosh, 2022.

ISBN 13: 978-93-93695-44-4
Published and Printed By
Country Girrl
Noel Lorenz House of Fiction
Headquarters - Kolkata, West Bengal, India
154A, KCG Road, Kolkata - 700050
www.noellorenz.com

Dedicated

To NLHFians.

Preface

Patch of Happiness is a book that depicts the writer's point of view of looking at life.

- Rubindeep Kaur

1 January 2022

Ludhiana, India

NLHF – The Publisher with All Free Books in World Records

Acknowledgements

- We want to thank all the writers who kindly contributed to this book.

- I want to thank my parents for all the time I was busy editing this book.

- I want to thank Goddess Saraswati for blessing me to be the editor of such a wonderful work of art.

-Noel Lorenz

I, the compiler, want to thank everyone who contributed to making this book. This book was nothing without the support of the writers. If the support of writers could not be obtained, all the efforts would have been sheer waste. The book depicts the writer's point of view of looking at life. Every writer shares his best experience of life to motivate people to look at the positive side of life. Not only the writers but publication should also be thanked for their publishing efforts.

- Rubindeep Kaur

Contents

Rubindeep Kaur

COMPILER

NLHF – The Publisher with All Free Books in World Records

Rubindeep kaur is a passionate writer. She is an 18-year-old girl and a resident of Punjab. She recently passed out her class 12. Her hobbies are painting and drawing, reading and writing. She took part in many anthologies. She also compiled an anthology. She likes writing and presenting thoughts on a piece of paper. She is the compiler of this book. According to her, a patch of happiness means things that make us happy and memories are one of them.

Website: www.noellorenz.com   Fb/Insta/Twitter: @noellorenzbooks

Memories: present too becomes past

Memories link us to a nearly forgotten past,

The time went away too fast,

We count on our memories

when the past seems to be better than the present,

Our mind and brain is the bridge between the past and present,

Those flashbacks relieve the boredom of today,

My heart, my body and whole self feels nostalgic,

Longing for those days to return,

My eyes shed tears on remembering a good day,

But still accepting the today,

Because present will also become past,

These roses of pleasure will too fade away,

Childhood would turn into adulthood one day,

So enjoy your present to the fullest

@rubindeep @robi_writer

Some people share their experiences with you,

Some people create their experiences with you,

I also got some people in my life,

They separated my heart from the buried knife,

Old people may have treated you as a friend,

New people may treat you as a family member till the end,

© Rubindeep Kaur

Hindi writers

Sikha Ojha

My name is Shikha Ojha. I belong to Gorakhpur. I don't write a word. I write feeling of world.

मनमानी

क्या करे क्या ना करें,

हम यू गुमसुम क्यू रहे

नाचो गाए खेलेंगे हम

मस्ती में हरपल झूमेंगे हम,

आओ करें थोड़ी शैतानी,

बारिश के पानी करे मनमानी,

क्या करे क्या ना करें,

हर पल क्यू गुमसुम रहे,

आओ खुलके हसलो तुम

भूल जाओ सारे गम

ना करो यू आंखे नम,

छोड़ो अब दुनिया की बाते

देखो जैसे तारे टिमटिमाते,

हर पल रहो बस हसते गाते,

छोड़ो सब की बाते

आओ करे हम बस मनमानी

बारिश के पानी खूब शैतानी,

करते रहो बस मनमानी

Nidhi Khandelwal

मेरा नाम निधि खंडेलवाल है। मैं एक गृहिणी हूँ। मुझे नई नई चीजों के बारे में जाना अच्छा लगता है।मैं खुद की पहचान बनाना चाहती हूँ। मुझे वैसे तो शायरी लिखनी नहीं आती है और ना ही लिखना मेरा शौक है। बस मैं दिल की बातों को,जज्बातो को खुद से मिलवाना चाहती हूँ। दिल की हसरतें तो बहुत है मगर अभी खुद को खुद से नई पहचान देना बाकी है।

यादें- कुछ नयी पुरानी

आज भी यादें कुछ नयी कुछ पुरानी याद आती हैं

इन यादों में अब भी उनकी बातें याद आती हैं

कभी हार के हमने हार ना मानी थी

कभी जीत की खुशियाँ उनके साथ बाँटी थी

वो दिन भी कोई कैसे भूल जा सकता हैं

जिनके साथ कभी अपना बच्पन जिया करते थें

आज भी यादों में उन्हीं के रहा करते हैं

काश लौट आते वो बीते दिनों के दिन

जिनमें फिर से जी लेते हम उन बीते दिन

खो कर जिन यादों को आज हम जी रहे हैं

हम उनको अपने सपनों में सी रहे हैं

हर लम्हा यूँ बेजान परिंदे सा जी रहे हैं।

Insta id : Nidhi 779

Ankita Nahar

AKII#@@@ अंकिता न हार मुल्य रूप से अजमेर राजस्थान की रहने वाली है। वाली हैं। ये ललखने के ललए हमेशा उत्साहहत रहती है साथ ही हमेशा वह सब्दो से सकुना चाहती है। ये अपने विचारो और जो भी इन्होंने अपनी जनजदगी से सीखा है, अनभु व ल्लाल्या है, उसे अपनी रचनाओं मे लिख देती है। इससे उनकी रचनाएं बहुत ही ज्यादा भाव और प्रभावशाली बन जाती ह

हदन वो भी कमाल के

के वो भी बडे गजब के थे

जब घर परिवार को छोड़ कर के एक अलग ही दुनिया में आ गये थे

अपने घर में अपने कमरे की बात

और हाउसिंग ke कमरे ki बात में रात दिन का अंतर था,

और सही बताऊं को सच में

शुरू शुरू में यहा रहना थोड़ा मुश्किल हो गया था,

पर धीरे धीरे इसकी इतनी

गनदी आदत कब हो गई की
घर लौट आने का भी मन होता था पर लौट आने मे भी ज़ोर लगता था,
ये सब कब कैसे हो गया

पता ही नहीं चला

दोस्तो के साथ की गयी,

रात भर की बाते हो या

किसी एक दोस्त के साथ शमलकर

दूसरे दोस्त की वात लगनी हो,

ये तो रोज़ का किस्सा हो गया था,

ना जाने अब एसे कितने ही

ही हस्सी के किससे हो

जो अब याद आया करते है

THIS WORLD
FULL of HOPE
BEGIN T
PROCEED

English writers

Mohammad Majid Khan

This Is Mohammed Majid Khan urf Mmk writer Writing is his passion and He is a retail professional working as as a Category champion at Reliance.He Get Time for his True Writing His own Words from His Busy life So that the words could touch everyones hearts.

Unki Yaaden Jaise Mujhme Basi h

1.

Kal Raat Kuch Aysaa hua Ankhen Nam hui, Yeh Kaisa Toofan aya Ke Unki Yaaden Taza hui, Soncha Kayi Saal Hue Na Meri Unse Baat hui Na hi Mulakhat hui, Aur Pata bhi Na Chala Na Jane Kab adhi Raat hui, Hum Yaad me unki Gum the Aur Shaher bhar me Jhum ke Barsaat hui

2.

Bhi Pata Nahi Chalta hai, Mai Kisme, Mujhme Koun Rehta Hai, Sargoshiyaan uski Gehre Rehti Hai, Dur Hoke Bhi Judaa Kaha Rehta Hai, Sulagte Rehte Hai khud Ke Andar, Haal Apna Koun Kisi Se Kehta Hai, Tu Kehta Hai Tera Thikana Nahi Mai, Toh Woh Koun Hai Jo Mujhme Rehta Hai, Dhundta Phirta Hun Jane Kabse Khud ko, Ab Pata Chala Mai Kaha Rehta Hun, Logg Samjhte Hai Sannata fahela Hai, Nahi Smjhte Ke Yeh Kya- Kya Kehta Hai, Hum Toh Naam Bhar Ke Fakat Hai Shayar, Asal Toh Woh Hai Joh Mujhme Rehta Hai...

Insta I'd : mmk._. writer

Abhipsa Lenka

Abhipsa Lenka is living in Bhubaneswar, Odisha and was born on 2nd November 2001 at Bhubaneswar, Odisha. She is pursuing diploma in electrical engineering in government polytechnic, Bhubaneswar. She was not a professional writter bt she became passionate in writing quotes and poems.

Memories

Timeless treasures of the heart.

Memories

Be with us forever Memories

Give us happiness Memories

Meant to be remembered for whole life.

Memories

Things pass but by capturing the precious moments we had.

Memories

Hoping to see someone again.

Memories

Creating new ones with adding old ones.

Memories

This is the only thing no one can change it.

Memories

Never end Endless story of our life time journey.

Abhiram

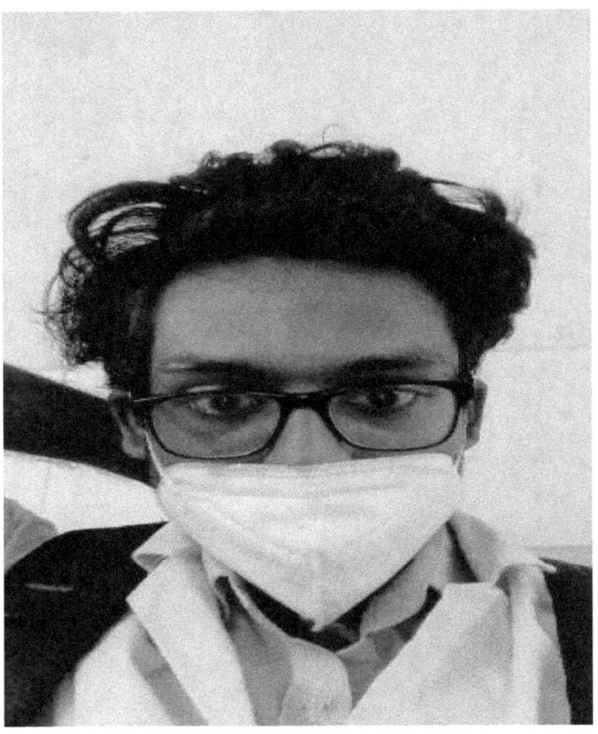

Hailing from Alleppey, Kerala; and a medical student in GMC (RIMS), Ongole, Andhra Pradesh, Abhiram is a technology freak, and likes reading, writing, travelling, listening to songs and watching movies. He likes writing whatever it comes to his mind, and likes writing poems, stories, microtales and motivational quotes. He has written 30+ anthologies as a co-author, and is compiling a few ones too. He is the founder of the writing community Spread Those Inks. He is the National Record Holder for the compilation of the anthology "Soul in the glass."

<u>THOSE MEMORIES.</u>

I have been living in solace.

With no one with me, even to talk.

But haven't I been a part of many events,

Which made my memories with them?

I haven't forgotten completely How they were to me,

But now I feel How I enjoyed them so much.

Like the molecule of flowing air,

It comes and goes, without notice. But the memory it leaves behind,

That becomes valuable, And I can't forget it,

Even when Parkinson's disease,

Or amnesia; Starts on me,

Because all positive memories I remember,

Are all gold for me, And I want to enjoy again.

<u>MEMORIES WITH YOU</u>

You are far now, from me; And I feel the wind everytime. ,
The presence of the shining spirit Which always reveals that
is you.

We have many memories in us,

All with love and romance,

But haven't been you sad,

When I left for an emergency?

I want to meet you back.

And fill that aching heart of yours,

With the medicine called "love."

That would be the best memory of our relationship

Mr. Augash Partiban

Mr. Augash Parthiban was born in Chennai, TamilNadu on May 09 in the year of 2000 and he has graduated in Bachelor of Commerce specialized in Department of Accounting and Finance from Madras University and still pursuing MBA from NMIMS University Bangalore. He

is a passionate writer tooo

Hey Sister? Hello Christmas!

We are here for you Dear! To celebrate your day!!!

Hahaha.....!!!! Hahaha.   !!!!

During childhood days obviously me and my sister, Habitual of counting the christmas stars in the houses! While we returned back from the tuition by night time.....

Can't forget those memories!!

Because if the Christmas comes those days to be remembered still   Love You Christmas!!!

Paint may erase or fade often! But, Memories never fade".

Memories may bring back to the mind often

Friendly Questions with Funny Answers, But Made It as MemOries

Hey ya!!

My friends asked me, are you single are committed?

I said…

Yes, I'm committed!!

Is it?

Yeah!!! Yeah!!!

I'm committed with my family and friends.

Oh I see

Love forever towards family and friends.

"Never forget those memories, that too these kind of questions like Single or committed in friends circle"

Friends Forever!! Love Forever!! Ever! Ever

B. L. Sai Saranya

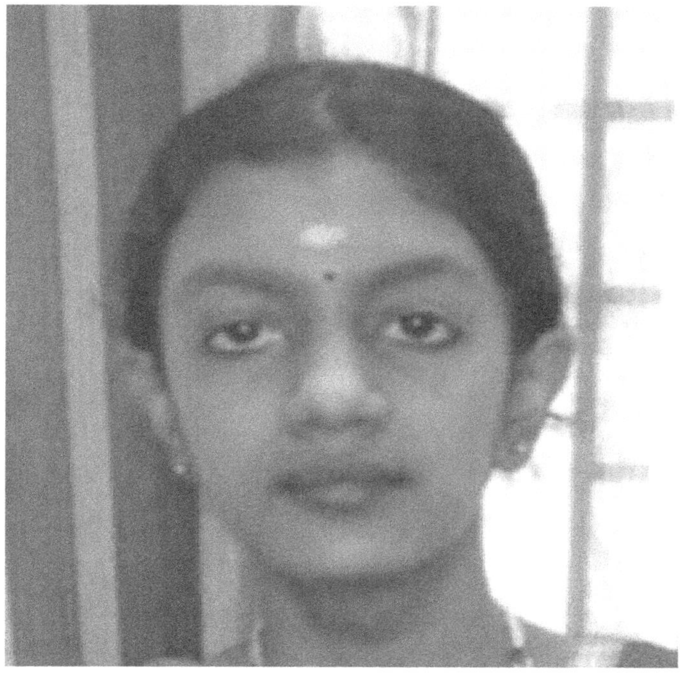

Name: B. L. Sai Saranya. Class: 9th B.

School: Kendriya Vidyalaya No 1 Tirupati. Hobbies: Reading books, playing and singing.

Memories are treasuries

Memories are treasuries,

Which come and go

But they always stay

In our hearts and souls.

Sometimes memories bring happiness

Sometimes they bring sadness.

But whenever we recall our memories,

we dwell into the past.

Memories come along with us throughout our life like a journey partner because we cannot forget them forever.

Memories cannot be seen Memories cannot be captured Memories can be stolen

Because they are stored in our hearts.

Charitha Sree Pillai

Mis.Charitha Sree Pillai.K of 18years was born to smt. Suneetha and Sri Ramesh on 28th of April. Currently persusing bachelor degree in mechanical engineering from JNTUACE KALIKIRI.she paid intrest over literature at a young age. More over she is a classical dancer(bharathanatyam)

Insta I'd:i_proxima

Pen name :proxima

<u>Memories of u...</u>

There was a time .....

still I remember,

I left with nothing,

Not even an inch of hope,

Nor to trust anymore..

My eyes are out of tears,

Walking alone in the lane,

Cursing the Lord for putting me into this,

Praying for a miracle to happen..

I was at the edges,

No words to express my sorrow,

Reached the peaks of insults,

Seen the depth of guilt..

I had forgot to laugh heartfully,

I'm out of words to speak openly,

Every word of others cutted my veins internally..

I never raised my voice

nor opened my mouth,

But the supreme has listened my words..

He solved this matrix in the form of "U"

You made every movement a memory,

Thanks for adding joy to my happiness, colours to my life,

For making my eyes shine, heart to smile and eyes twinkle....

-proxima

Bhimesh

Mr. Bhimesh, teacher by profession, serves as an English teacher at Kendriya Vidyalaya, Tirupati. He has adopted writing poems and stories as his passion and also guide his students in acquiring these skills. he has published many of his poems in various anthologies.

<u>Then and Now</u>

Child I was then,

My Father's shoulder: a caravan.

He gave me rides, What a healing fun!!

Oh!! I am now a young lad Took a flight!!

My father's delight

But I say! Flights never match with rides.

School going boy I was,

My mother's treasure was bit a free,

She gave two bits and patted and smiled I ate candies and be merry all those days.

Earning now lakhs,

Gave my mom a pack of notes.

My mother's delight.

But I say!! Pack of notes never match with those bits.

Blue sky, cool air-

Can't forget my cropped hairs.

Games were plenty and so my friends!

Days were spent like in heaven...

Alas! Those days are dead.

Numerous followers in all the platforms,

Yet alone under roof.

So I say! Followers never match with those friends.

@Chinnu Bhimesh

Bruhati

I am Bruhati. Writing fictional, mysterious and life based poems is my hobby and I want to continue this as my passion.

Purity in hardship

Starting with a small story,

To end up seeing the stars. Going to the school with joy,

And come back as drained. Doing homework for playing,

Then sleeping for dreaming tales.

People taunt everyone,

We try to prove them wrong,

But none of us try to be self!

Everyone wish to be rich

But no one to be kind,

The real richness is being yourself and being kind to others.

Be kind then you are also rich! We start up doing something,
But end up doing something else.

World is running behind time,

But time never run behind anyone!

Each and everyone is precious,

But we never recognize them!! When we recognize others,

The world will start recognizing you.

B. V. Vanshika

Miss. B.V. Vansika of class 9 studying in Kendriya Vidyalaya No 1 Tirupati, AP has begun her literary journey through this publication. She has passionated of being a published poet a long ago. Her hobbies include drawing, reading short stories etc. Wishing her a great literary journey.

My Sweet memories

Down the lane when I look back

The memories of my school days flash back

Everything was so lovely

Everything was so cheerful

The blooming flowers in the spring

And playing with friends on the swings

Gone are those days sharing food

With friends in lunch

Cracking jokes and playing pranks

In back bench

Missing you all my lovely

friends Teachers and school

The memories of you all are so

Thrilling and so cool

Waiting to see you very soon

Praying to God

Every morning every noon

Memories remind us of our actions

Each of which is an experience.

Memories contribute valuable life lessons

That teach us to live with better sense.

Chaitra

Chaitra is a Passionate Writer. She completed her education in Navodaya from 6th to 12th. And now she is studying B.Sc. (CBZ) second year Degree in Gadag. Her hobbies are Reading novels, Writing, and collecting ornaments.

<u>NAVODAYA - The Heaven</u>

The juvenile soul......

Set foot into the unknown land

At first, everything was strange

Then, he met many such souls

And now they are his Buddies

He felt the syllabus was quite tough

As the days passed.....

Teachers supported, guided and taught him

Their parental love provided for him

He worked hard....

The syllabus was easy.....

He enjoyed every moments there

Junior senior bond was covalent

House spirit, class spirit was extremely high

During the competitions, sports and Cultural nights.....

The little fights with Classmates

Leadership, funny moments, irritations, ragging Imitations,
morning and evening PET session

Interesting and boring speeches, library, music hall

Comdey moments during assembly, meditation, yoga classes

Did some mischievous things in dormetry etc.....

Lot of emotions with this Campus

This happy Land was heaven for NAVODAYANS.....

Now, missing all the Teachers and Campus badly.

@Ammu.vj.chai2426

Chandan

Chandan is an accountant and has just started his journey in writing. He likes to read, exercise and doing yoga .

Insta id : @Shalomamanthakur159753

<u>Childhood memories</u>

It was the day of a festival In our near by village

I went early to the festival As I was super excited

It was a Great pleasure For

Me to join And have An insight into that Religious festival
That was my greatest

.Positive memory Till date That day , I felt that

I never had such an Experience In my whole life I felt Love
for

Everything I saw

Chris Korten

Christopher Korten is Professor of History and Director of Academic Writing at MGIMO University, Moscow and Adam Mickiewicz University, Poznan, Poland. This is his first poem. @chris.korten

<u>Memories are like Lives</u>

Memories are lives lived at your convenience within the confines of your mind.

You direct, produce and often act in them. They connect you to a nearly forgotten past.

But that moment of eternal neglect is delayed by the emergence of your fondest recollections, yearning to be relived or at least relished,

One Last Time.

Happy memories are moments best remembered and then, whether we desire it or not, unceremoniously forgotten.

Jannat

Jannat was born on 20 February 2003.she is in 12th standard, she has also recited a poem 'bhai' and scored the second position in commerce talent search competition when she was in 11th standard. Her hobbies are watching movies and web series, reading novels and listening to music.

Blow of remembrance

Often, in my throwback streets, I wonder,

Perceiving over those days,

Every time I go there I wonder,

Such a boon I feel in this phase,

It is a hallucination of solicitude intense,

Because it's a blow of remembrance.......

Such a jovial company is given to me by memories,

For me, these are sweet, fragrant flowers,

Overpowering and overwhelming natural powers,

A vast ground with a lake of influence,

Yes for me it's a blow of remembrance......

Whenever my conscious was engulfed by memories,

And I become jocund and half melancholic,

At that time I used to hate my solicitude enemies

Who made me ill-tempered, hyper and sick,

Let anyone harm my solicitude I couldn't give a chance,
Cause it's a blow of remembrance.....

Now I know that memories

It has the power to take us to our past,

Refreshing our minds and peaceful sighs,

And keeps our youth to last.

Kashish Chawla

Kashish Chawla is a passionate writer. She loves reading novels. She is doing her She wanted to become a well known author. She is pursuing her secondary education from Sacred Heart Convent School.

Insta id :@Its_kashish_chawla

<u>People move on but memories stay</u>

"Throughout life you will meet one person who is like no other."

Me and my best friend (Sabgun) use to spend our quality time together. Once I went to her home for preparing notes. Her mother was not at home and we both felt hungry. We searched for something to eat but just found biscuits and a pack of maggie. Though we were two, we had just one packet of maggie. So we decided to busy ourself till her mother comes. We started clicking selfies. We started walking in the park which was behind her house. We found a puppy in the park who was wounded. We took her at home and provided proper medication and she gave milk in a bowl to him. We both felt condolence at him. She decided to keep it with her. We started playing with it and just forgot everything we were doing or feeling. After a week I got the worst news that my best friend Sabgun left me alone.

Yes, she died. Though we made a lot of memories, the best moment for both of us was the day we met that puppy as we both laughed and enjoyed enough.

People come and go but memories always stay in our mind.

Still can't forget the time I spent with her. She is always with me in my heart.

Lika Kauridze

Lika Kauridze is person who writes poem. She is from Georgia, number 22 public school pupil

Insta id :@likaliko123456789

<u>A patch of happiness</u>

The happiness is a combination of how satisfied you are with your life, but unfortunately we can not recognise some details what can makes us happier.

In this topic I want to tell you my experience, how some happiness changed my life.

When I was sixteen years old I had a lots if problems, that was bad period in my life when med my sweetheart broke up, I did not have money, I had problems in school and this everything was so painful and caused my depression.

So it was cleared that I need to wake up. In this period my brother was formula of happiness, with this person I recognised a lot of things, I learn a lot and I developed.

Everything happened ones when it was summer's hot day, I was standing in front of the window at night and I was looking at the moon and I thought that only it could have heard me, at this moment my brother come into room and stood next to me, he said me "I know you are much beautiful when you are smiling"

I looked at him and smiled, then he continues "just smile whatever because life is quiet short to lose your brilliant time and problems, oh, problems are so good chance to change something in you," I did not know what to reply him and I just said that it was difficult but he smiled me and said that he understood everything but only yourself could helped me.

This words were the best thing at this moment and I was bit happy and all night I thought about it. He made me sure of my own strength and he gave me motivation to never give up despite the resistance.

Muskan

Muskan is a student of class 12. She loves reading books, dancing, singing. Writing poems is also one of her hobby. She has a lot of dreams and she wants to achieve a lot of success in her life.

<u>My temple of 15 years</u>

You are lucky to hear

But my journey of fifteen years.

It was a long path

Where I faced a lot of wraths.

The temple is my school,

Which used to have so many rules.

Though I went lonely inside

But came out with many rules and rights.

Every year I stepped ahead

With new books and a new head.

That ring-a- ring-a roses

With beautiful poses.

That yellow sunshine

On faces nine,

Will remain always in my mind,

Learned many eating trends

In the middle of periods,

With my friends.

Can't forget that tears of my eyes

When my teachers scoldings,

Turns out as an advice.

Navya

She is Navya. She is a HR Generalist, A Writer, Poetess, Blogger, Podcaster. She is the Founder of Merakians, A Community under Inkzoid Foundation, Co founder of Spread Those Ink's, Words of Wisdom. S.

Insta id:@thoughtsofnavs_

<u>School Memories</u>

The feeling of going back to school seems oh so surreal

Those carefree days and stress free days

Which everyone needs to remember is sometimes forgotten by us.

Those group studies which we had with our friends

Those meet ups, bunking school etc,

Those first love memories

Those canteen snaps, those memorable moments.

Those festival celebrations, birthdays that we celebrate with our friends

Oh they make us all so nostalgic

And take us down memory lane

Never forget your school memories!

~Navya

College Memories

I still remember my college UG farewell

Like a fresh memory.

That day was a bittersweet day.

How I wish I relive those memories once again.

Three years of Ug life was the best thing ever.

How I wish those memories are re lived again.

I am really nostalgic writing this.

Writing this makes me go down memory lane.

Cherish your college memories.

And make your life magical and worth living.

Memories aren't forgotten.

They are to be remembered for ages to come

Nisarga

Nisarga is a girl who has ambitions of becoming a doctor, she studies in class 12th, and she is interested in dance, reading novels, writing.

Insta id:@Nisarga_hiregoudar_03

CHILDHOOD MEMORIES

My mother tells me about it, But I remember a little bit.

Those are the days, When I was so innocent.

It was the most precious thing in life.

When life was exciting and alluring.

Those are the days,

Which are passed and never come back.

The thought recalling of my childhood

Always cheers up my mood.

Those are the days

Which are unforgettable of mine.

That was the time when,

I used to play with my toys, And my life,

Filled with happiness and joy.

I will wish to become smart and good

But, my first preference will be my childhood.

Pranjal Jain

Pranjal Jain was born on 21st May, 2002 in Howrah, West Bengal in India. She got her early education in Howrah afterwards which her family shifted to Ludhiana where she completed her schooling from Sacred Heart Convent School. Pranjal pursues many hobbies such as listening music, sketching, cooking and writing poems. She started writing poems as a stress buster for her which actually turns out to be one of her inborn interest.

Memories: Go Back

When I walk down my memory lane, My heart aches in pain.

Beautiful past flashes across my mind, Requesting the harsh realities to be on me kind.

Suddenly strikes the reality, Showing me my life in brutality.

No way to be rescued,

Telling my heart , "the memories be pursued."

When I close my eyes, I see all the pretty faces who crossed me to rise.

Giving my struggle their own share and size.

Suddenly 'today' touches me and I see the light, Showing me my life in the bright.

My heart tells me, "No reason to be sad, What was destined to happen have already had."

See the light , move forward.

Behave brave and bold and not as a coward.

Memories sometimes soothes us,sometimes hurt.

Sometimes pulls us back and sometimes help us to revert.

"BUT ALL IS WELL THAT ENDS WELL"

Priyanka

I am Priyanka in 10th standard in Kendriya Vidyalaya No 1 Tpt. My hobbies are dancing, writing poems and stories.

School memories (that's school)

SCHOOL MEMORIES

The pressure of expectations

Expected to behave when u all you want to do is fool around
Expected to score A's when you are too lazy to study
Expected to listen in class when all you want to do is gossip
That's school ...

Biggest fear of loosing friends The friends who we love

The countless jokes and laughs The countless fun times The
countless memories

That's school ...

In the morning we don't want to go At the end of the day, you
are glad You did

The lessons learned and the good times You realise school is
not so bad

Having to listen to lectures Having to do work when all you
Want to do is sleep

That's school ...

Rumi

Rumiyati Rasmin is publishing her first write-up. She was born on 03 May in Indonesia.Her hobbies are cooking and reading books. She is a teacher by profession.

Happiness

Life is short

Beautiful only imagination.

Every single person will keep on their mind.

And will find their happiness.

With different way.

Darkness, lightness will come.

Feel bless, lucky and sometime unlucky.

Up and down will come through our life.

Weakness and strongest come in the Family, friends
and neighbour come to our life.

Have them we can chat any kind of problem that we have.

They will accompany us, during difficult time.

You will find some of them will true and honestly to you.

Yes, this is a life.

Happiness come into our life but not of them make us feel
happy.

S. Gokulsaai

He is S. Gokulsaai, studying 9th in Kendriya Vidyalya No.1 Tirupathi and his Hobbies are Learning New things, Creating New things.

<u>Memories</u>

Memories

Remember!!all the beautiful times.

The first times, The Emotions,

The excitement.

Remember the colours.

The Smell of Friendship, The trust.

A Holiday in the Summer.

One heart is running with lots of idea's.

And remember the Memories.

Some Memories are very Sweet.

And some may not you don't focus

And don't think of that focus on your

Goal and continue, your journey of life.

The Good memories bring you

A Good Friend, A Good Society,

The Good Conditions.When Good memories are with you.

Some bad memories will disturb your concentration, your focus, and

you will lose

Your Friend, society, good conditions.

So, when you turn back after completing all

Tasks.

You may see all Good memories only.

One or two bad memories are common

Throw it on the Dust bin and continue your life.

"NOW CLOSE YOUR EYES AND REMEMBER

WHAT THE FUN AND SAD YOU HAD IN

YOUR LIFE."

Shivapriya

Miss. Shivapriya Hiremath from Gadag- Karnataka has writing poems as her passion. She portrays her feeling through her words of poetry. Her goal is to make her poetry and narrations as an asset for her lifetime. Dreams are in her mind and are well expressed by her hand.

@raised_by_strong_woman

IN THE MEMORY OF YOU

The day I stepped on to this earth,

I did not know how lucky I was.

But the day I take my last breath,

Surely there will be a curve in my face.

It's just because how lucky Am I?

To had such a blessing in my life like YOU.

You never asked me for the great ranks,

But taught me how to lead the life.

You never blamed me for my mistakes,

But alerted me to never repeat it.

It's just like, I'm blessed with the eyes,

But my beautiful vision was YOU.

I had never felt hungriness,

As you ever nurtured me with great nutrients.

I had never felt to take amiss,

As you never even trained me to surmise.

And Now the path am walking on,

Is the way designed by YOU.

Everybody stays yet an empty house,

Everyone uses yet an empty chair.

Many love me yet an empty heart,

Your touch, kisses, talks no longer there.

Everything said above, left as Memories

YOU will always be missed DADDY.

-Shivapriya Hiremath

K Siddartha Pillai

Mr. Siddartha Pillai is studying in class 10th in Kendriya Vidhyalaya. He got his interest in poems after he wrote a poem on Stephen Hawking for which he received appreciation. From then he started writing poems. He then developed a great love for poetry.

<u>Golden life</u>

The days have grown longer I got away from u all

Since I remember all memories and

Time we spent together

It was a wonderful experience

It may be walking in group from school to home

I miss that group today

Now I go and come alone home

Or it maybe

Just walking around the ground of our school

After the school hours

Or maybe on the

Way, combining with a sweet chat

It may be fighting like stupids on the road

To roaring in our classroom

U all changed me from just a person

To a good human being

I miss our hangouts

I miss our combined studies just before

One night of exam

U helped me in my sorrows

U celebrated my happiness

- Passio

Soliha

Soliha Shafi Beigh is 23 years old and was born in Kashmir. Doing her masters in health and hospital administration from Jamia Hamdard, New Delhi. She loves to read and write.

Insta id:@shambledheart

<u>In our hearts forever</u>

You were the sunshine of my life

You nourished me with your utmost love!

Every time I miss your presence

Every second I miss your care!

I still remember how you always bought chocolates for me!

You put a space inside me Nobody can fill that place

I don't know how to live without you

But I am trying my best You will always be with us

Forever in my heart.

TEL:821377772

Anna

Vanishing memories

I wish I could be the rain droplets

Watching those raindrops fall

I put my face towards them

And feel the rain droplets

They took my pain away For a while…!

I could hear the rain laughing with joy!

It mesmerizes my inner feelings.

And somehow I get peace

I love to walk in the rain .

Thomalika

Thomalika keerthi kesani DOB:22-03-2003 listening to music, reading story books

Insta id: thomalikakeerthikesan

The pain that I feel every night,

Couldn't get it,

Through big smile face in the morning,

Do I wear a mask to the face?

Every memory makes me to do;

The reason I smile alone,

Is the reason of a joyful memory,

The reason I cry alone,

Is the reason of a tearful memory,

My heart breaks down,

My eyes are overwhelmed with water,

My heart may stop one day,

But my brain doesn'brain thinks and things,

My heart breaks and breaks.

I am grateful dead.

I could miss you everyday,

And still be glad, You are no more in my life,

But I have your memories

To smile and cry alone.

Yes I am grateful.

Vijaykumar

Vijayakumar is an outspoken person who is very passionate about learning. His hobbies are typewriting and dreaming. He attaches lot of importance to imagination because it is the root of innovation.

Finally, to say he is person with merit and spirit. Because merit without spirit is fruitless and spirit without merit is useless.

<u>PERSPECTIVES ON MEMORIES</u>

IN MIND WE ALL CARRY MEMORIES AS TEXT, IMAGES
AND STORIES NOT ALL OF THEM ARE SWEET

SOME MAKE OUR HEART FAST BEAT

A FEW GIVE PLEASANT FEELINGS OF FAR AS
OPPOSED SOME REMIND US OF DEEP SCAR

BOTH OF THEM BRING PAST TO PRESENT BUT THE
FEELINGS THEY EVOKE IS DIFFERENT

REMINISCENCES OF A SCHOOL GIRL BEGINS WITH
THE MORNING BELL FILLED WITH FUN AND
PLEASURE

THAT THEY HAD DURING THEIR LEISURE

RECOLLECTION OF PLEASANT PASTS IS LIKE GOLD
WHICH DOESN'T FADE AWAY WITH TIME AS OLD
THEY ARE ALWAYS FRESH AND GREEN

THAT THEY RUSH INTO OUR MIND SCREEN

MEMORIES OF A WAR SOLDIER IS TOO HEAVY TO
SHOULDER

FULL OF PAIN AND PRESSURE

Yashwant Saini

For you are a fragile Flower, And I am a silly fly lost in you, Honey!" A vagabond who unexpectedly finds his home in loveliest of all hearts. Under her influence! Yashwant witnessed some best years of his life. Where he learnt to let go darkness and chase light. Being fixed by the magic she carries within, Yashwant considers her a surpassing star, the source of optimism.

<u>My Best Memory</u>

Your smiling face remains the best memory.

My eyes ever captured.

<u>Till My Grave</u>

It was the tale of the times When our paths collided

It was then Darling!

All my roads became your heart destined.

Holding your hand, I realized That it fits well with mine.
You were the brightest star To my murky nights.

Time bought us together And it also made us fall apart.

Your departure doesn't hurt honey!

For you mercifully left these photographs.

I hope that you know,

I am grateful for all that I owe. I know it is cowardly- brave

For I will keep these pics till my grave.

Insta id : yashwant.saini_

Y. Khyathi

Y. Khyathi is studying class tenth in kendriya vidyalaya no 1
tirupati. She is born in vechalam Visakhapatnam Dt.
Andhra Pradesh. Her hobbies are reading books and
drawing.

<u>My village memories</u>

I have sweet memories of my village,

They are of my younger age.

We had three village fairs every year,

Where bull races are very fear.

My village is a green city not in words,

But it attracts colourful birds.

My village has a stream Sarada,

Which is as peaceful as Narmada

My village has a government school,

With full of strict rules.

My village has a stationary and medical shop,

With a satisfying raindrop.

We have our own house,

With a roaming mouse.

We don't have everything,

But we live like a king.

Children will be attracted to folk dances,

But not for the school classes.

I am also attracted to folk song.

They were so long.

The special village memories,

Will be with me for centuries.

I love my village very much,

Which gives me a pure touch.

Oliver Becker

Loaded with Midnight Memories

I watched our soul

dancing in the wintery breeze

Your lips, like a rose petal

Scented my breathe.

Your tiny eyes, that blinked all night,

like galactical sneeze.

And there, my grave stone

Will stand tall

Loaded with midnight memories.

colors of my heart

www.noellorenz.com